Book torn before 5/23/
2013

BROOMS ARE FOR FLYING!

by MICHAEL REX

SQUARE
FISH

Henry Holt and Company

To Karen,
for the whipped cream

SQUARE
FISH

An Imprint of Macmillan

Square Fish and the Square Fish logo are trademarks of Macmillan
and are used by Henry Holt and Company under license from Macmillan.

Library of Congress Cataloging-in-Publication Data
Rex, Michael. Brooms are for flying / by Michael Rex.
Summary: A group of young trick-or-treaters demonstrate that
"feet are for stomping," "eyes are for peeking," "mouths are for moaning,"
and "tummies are for treating." [1. Halloween—Fiction.] I. Title.
PZ7.R32875Br 2000 [E]—dc21 99-44493
ISBN: 978-0-312-38015-1

Originally published in the United States by Henry Holt and Company
Designed by Donna Mark
Square Fish logo designed by Filomena Tuosto
First Square Fish Edition: 2009
10 9 8 7 6 5 4 3 2 1
www.squarefishbooks.com

The artist used pencil and Adobe® Graphic Software
to create the illustrations for this book.

Everyone ready?
Follow me!

Legs are for marching.

Feet are for stomping.

Eyes are for peeking.

Arms are for reaching.

Wings are for flapping.

Tails are for wagging.

Bones are for shaking.

Capes are for sneaking.

Mouths are for moaning.

Tummies are for treating.

Masks are for . . .

. . . tricking.

And brooms are for flying.

Happy Halloween!